THIS WALKER BOOK BELONGS TO:

For my dearest Rikka

First published 1992
by Walker Books Ltd, 87 Vauxhall Walk
London SE11 5HJ

This edition published 1994

6 8 10 9 7 5

This book has been set in ITC Garamond.

Printed in Hong Kong

British Library Cataloguing in Publication Data
A catalogue record for this book is
available from the British Library.

ISBN 0-7445-3058-X

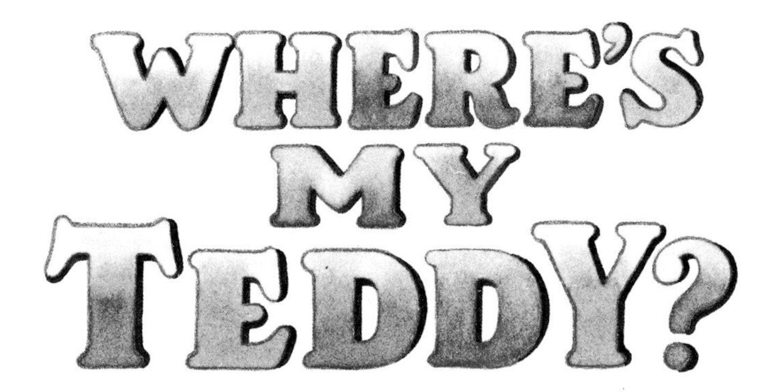

Jez Alborough

Eddy's off to find his teddy.
Eddy's teddy's name is Freddy.

He lost him in the wood somewhere.
It's dark and horrible in there.

"Help!" said Eddy. "I'm scared already!
I want my bed! I want my teddy!"

He tip-toed
on and on
until …

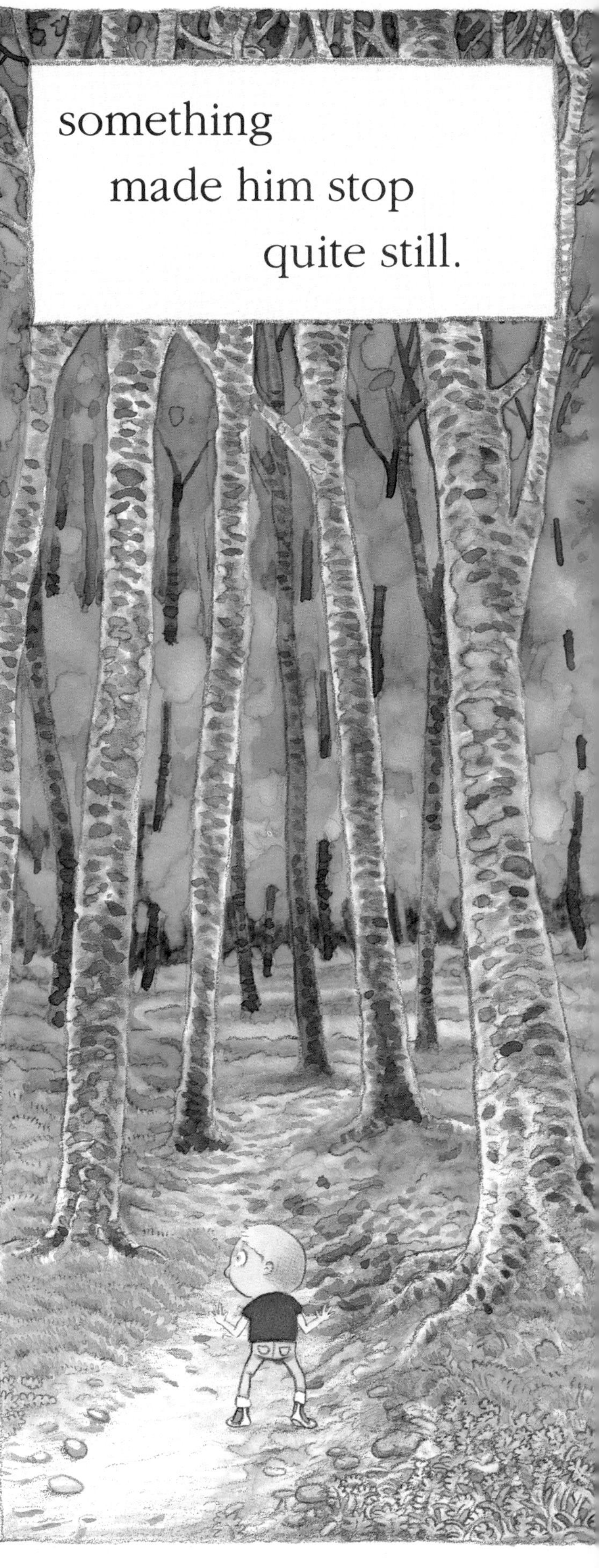
something
made him stop
quite still.

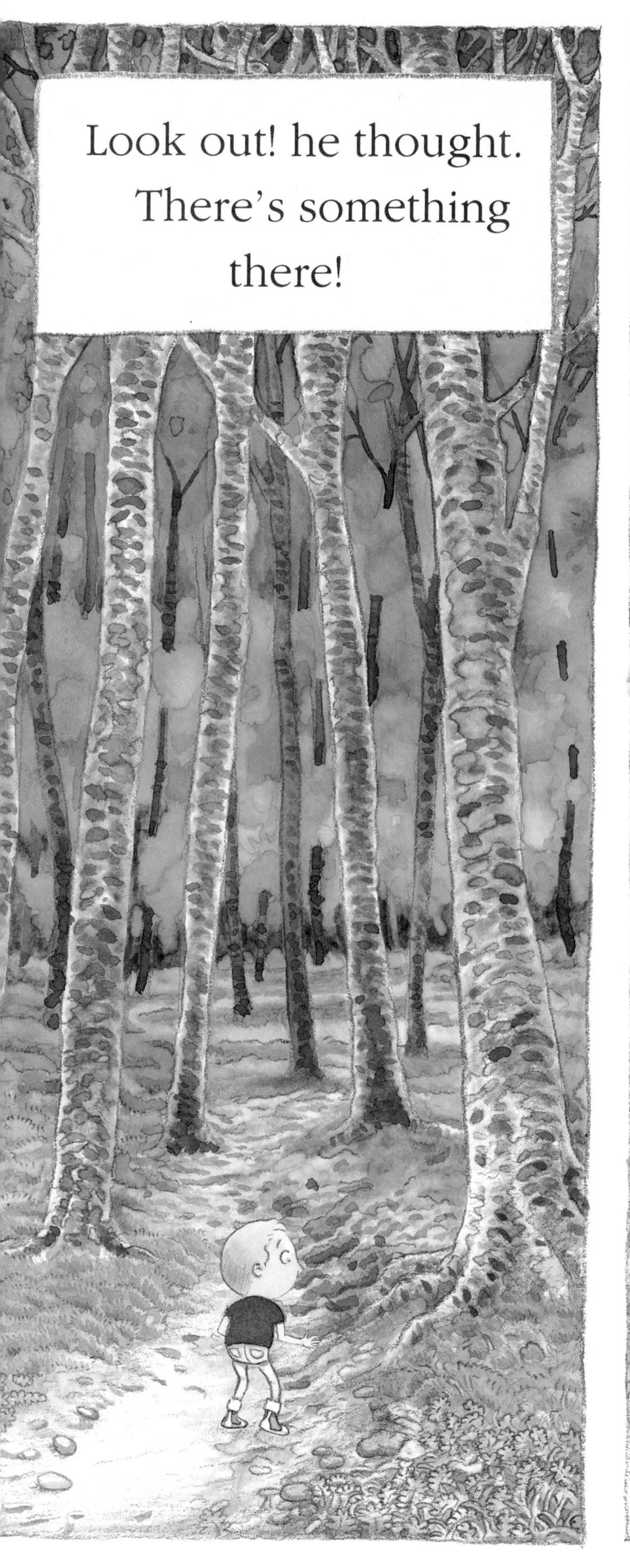
Look out! he thought. There's something there!

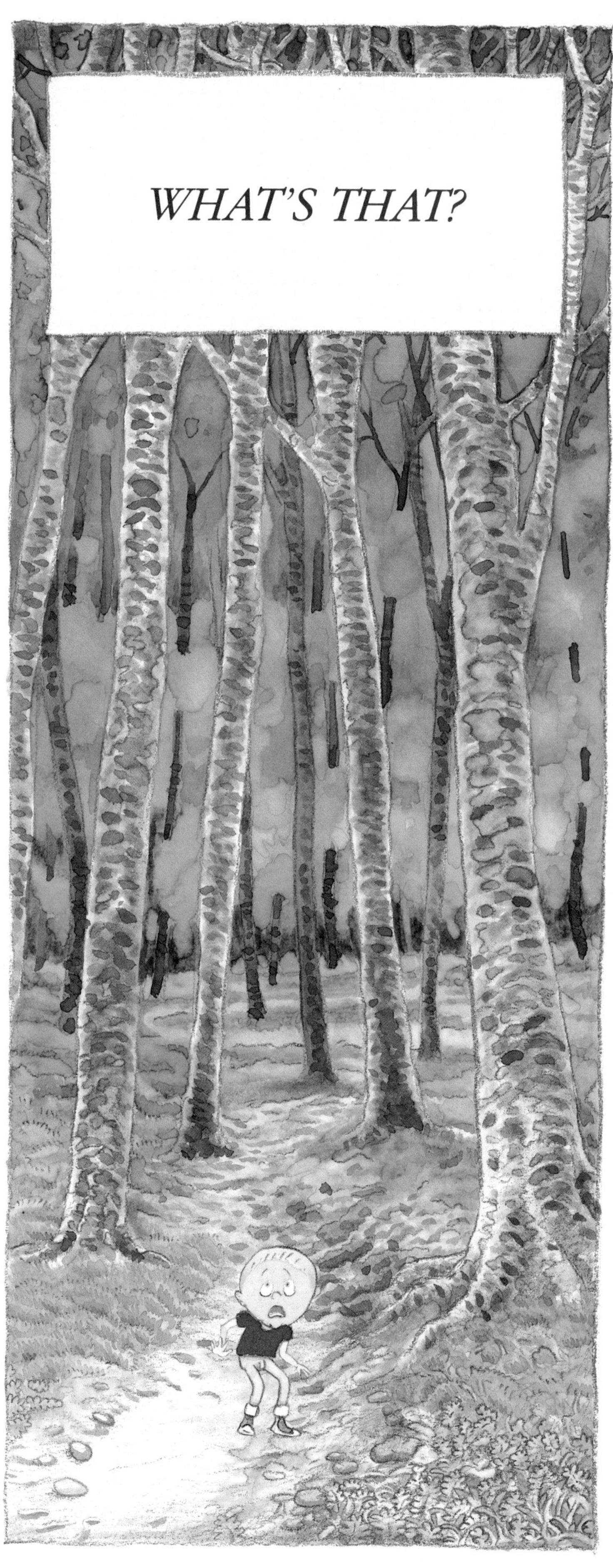
WHAT'S THAT?

A GIANT TEDDY BEAR!
"Is it Freddy?" said Eddy.
"What a surprise!
How *did* you get to be this size?"

"You're too big to huddle and cuddle," he said,

"and I'll never fit both of us into my bed."

Then out of the darkness,
clearer and clearer,
the sound of a sobbing
came nearer and nearer.

Soon the whole wood
could hear the voice bawl,
“How did you get to be
tiddly and small?
You’re too small to
huddle and cuddle,” it said,
“and you’ll only get lost
in my giant-sized bed!”

It was a gigantic bear
and a tiddly teddy
stomping towards …

the giant teddy and Eddy.

"MY TED!"
gasped the bear.
"A BEAR!"
screamed Eddy.

“A BOY!”
yelled the bear.
“MY TEDDY!”
cried Eddy.

Then they ran and they ran
through the dark wood
back to their homes
as quick as they could …

all the way back
to their snuggly beds,
where they huddled
and cuddled their
own little teds.

MORE WALKER PAPERBACKS
For You to Enjoy

Also by Jez Alborough

ESTHER'S TRUNK

Esther feels a proper chump,
Because her trunk has lost its trump.
The cause is strange and that's for sure,
But stranger still is the doctor's cure!

"Very funny." *Jennifer Taylor, British Book News*

0-7445-1493-2 £4.50

CUPBOARD BEAR

Lazy bear just loves to dream
Of his favourite thing – ICE-CREAM!
But bear's sweet dream turns to sour nightmare,
When he finds one day his cupboard's bare!

0-7445-1731-1 £3.99

BEAKY

The intriguing and irresistible tale of a rain-forest bird's search for his identity.

"Lots of ecological detail." *The Times Educational Supplement*

0-7445-1789-3 £3.99